11 SCENES

OCTAVIA JENSEN

ISBN: 9798842095551

The Discussion

Harrison Fucking Stag.

If someone told me three weeks ago I'd be walking up to his house to go over our BDSM checklists, I'd have called them crazy. Out-of-this-*world* crazy. But something about our time in the elevator changed him. He wasn't the cold, unapproachable lawyer anymore. He was someone I knew I could trust. Someone who'd proven worthy of my trust.

It was hard not to fall into all of it the second we left that elevator, but Harrison was professional, thor-

ough, not someone to push something before its time. He'd taken me
on dates to get to know more about
each other, ensured we were fully
comfortable with each other before
ever deciding to truly travel down
that road.

The aftercare he gave after that
night we spent trapped still lived in
my head rent-free, and now that we
were finally taking that huge step toward our preferred dynamic, I was
nervous as hell.

Especially after he'd shown me
his sex room.

I knocked on his door nervously
and hugged my folder, then forced a
smile the second he yanked it open.
"This checklist was very detailed,
Sir."

"Did you expect anything less,
kitten?" He raised a single eyebrow
and let me in, then shut the door

behind me a little forcefully. "I was careful not to forget anything."

"I know, and I appreciate it. I feel like this is a talk meant for your office, but can we do it on the couch? With a drink maybe?" I knew he wouldn't judge me for being nervous, but I still attempted to play it off as I kicked off my shoes.

Without a word, he brought over two glasses and a bottle of my favorite wine, then sat next to me and touched my leg. "This isn't the only conversation we'll ever have about this, so just relax. It's not a test, it's not something you can pass or fail."

I nodded, taking the comfort offered and soaking it up. "Thanks. So you said it had been a while since you Dommed. How long?"

"Few years," he admitted. "Four years and seven months, to be exact. I've had partners since then, though."

"Can I ask why none of them became your subs?" I took a sip and pressed my glasses up the bridge of my nose, watching him closely.

"Cheater," he whispered, smiling so lightly I almost missed it. "You know that thing with the glasses makes me weak. To answer your question, I'm not a good fit for every sub, and vice versa. It's as simple as that. Today, I want to find out if we're a good fit."

I was nervous all over again. "And if we're not … does that mean we can't see each other anymore, or just that we can't enter into a BDSM relationship specifically?"

Harrison gently took my glass and set it down, then faced me fully and held my hands. "It means whatever we want it to mean, Briella. I've waited a decade for you. If you think I'm letting you go because your kinks aren't my kinks and mine

8

aren't yours, you're delirious. Tell me you understand."

I nodded, feeling the truth behind his words as he stared into my eyes. "I understand, Sir."

"Good girl. Then let's begin with something we already know. We discovered in the elevator that you have a particular liking for a mix of degradation and praise. I need lines, kitten. Limits."

"I don't think I have many lines as far as degradation goes, as long as I feel safe, which is where the praise comes in. I normally need more aftercare after some degradation, but otherwise I like it tossed in here and there in and out of bed. Is that what you mean, or like names I like?"

He glanced at my papers and shook his head. "That's all here. You did a good job, Briella. Mine are behind you, you should take some time to look over them and ask me

9

any questions you have. Then we'll go through yours."

I took my time reading his, enjoying the ridiculously amazing foot rub he was giving me and when I realized how aligned we really were I had to bite back a grin. "I haven't tried some of the things you have but I'm absolutely open all of them. Have you already tried all of them?"

"Most." He stopped what he was doing to focus on me again, then let out a slow breath. "Did you take the Plan B pill last time?"

"Jumping right in there, huh? I was going to ease my way there. I … I did. But I had assumed it was a scene. Can we go into that more?"

He nodded, but I didn't miss the way his shoulders tensed. "I need you to understand something above everything else, Briella. You will always … always be the one in true control of your body. I would never attempt to take that from you. So yes, when I tell you not to take the pill or to get off your birth control, it's what I want, but I would never dream of forcing you. It may seem like I am when we're in a scene, but you will always be the one in true control. One word from you will stop me in my tracks."

I nodded, letting myself take in the lines of his strong jaw and how perfect his lips were. I couldn't handpick someone better to procreate with if I tried. "Okay, Sir. So outside of a scene, you wouldn't be upset if I ended up pregnant?"

"As I said, that's sort of my best-case scenario. But what kind of a man would I be if I forced you into that?" he asked. "You asked me why some of my previous partners weren't my subs. It's because I would've had to take control from them, and I won't do that. I need

11

you to willingly give yourself to me."

Something about him told me I could, that I could trust him with me fully and although I'd never given myself to someone like that before, deep down I wanted to. I was sick of having to be in control all the time, sick of having to pretend I could carry everything on my shoulders without a limp, because I couldn't. Sometimes I just needed to breathe. "How do we get to that point?"

"Carefully," he said with a soft laugh. "First, we finish going through our lists, then we get tested. What happened in the elevator happened because we thought we were dying, but we're not dying anymore, kitten. It's time to live."

I bit my lip, wanting to ride him right there on his couch, but I knew Harrison wouldn't cut any corners

JENSEN

here. That wasn't the type of man he was, and that was why I truly knew I was ready.

Edging

I awoke to his tongue sliding up my most precious area, making me gasp and spread for more. I loved this, loved how much attention and care he gave to me every time we were together, and when I remembered we were going to play today, my eyes darted open. I was finally going to see how bossy this man could really be. "Best way to wake up ever."

"We'll see how you feel in five minutes. You're not permitted to come, kitten. Not until tonight."

JENSEN

He pinned my legs open and sucked my clit, making me groan loudly. "Tonight? What time is it?" *Please tell me it's late as hell.*

"Quarter to seven," he said, pulling back just enough to slap my pussy. "The sun just came up. Now stop asking questions, I was busy."

Those fingers slid inside of me rougher than they had before, and I arched off the bed. I could do this, I'd edged before, but all day with him doing shit like that?

It was going to be a challenge.

I did, however, stop asking questions, and I took what he gave me until I was shaking with the need to let go.

"Good girl," he whispered, kissing my thighs and up my body to my lips. "Wear a skirt today. At eleven thirty, I'll call you up to my office. Make sure no one sees you."

I growled in frustration as I nodded. "Yep. Comfortable skirt, eleven thirty." He let me calm down before he helped me stand, and then I kissed him. "What panties should I wear, Sir?"

"That part is up to you." He kissed me again, holding my chin to keep me there until he was satisfied. "Start thinking about how my good girl would like to come tonight."

For a while, it was all I thought about. It helped me take the new elevator faster than before, made me zone out in a meeting thinking, and when eleven rolled around, I still hadn't decided. Did I want to come on his face, on his cock, on his thigh in his suit before he got to change?

I wanted all of the above.

"Earth to Briella," a loud voice interrupted my thoughts, making me gasp and snap the pencil I was using.

"What the hell, Grant?"

"You were zoning out and biting your lip. It was kinda hot, honestly," he said, stepping a little closer. "What were you thinking about?"

"Your sister. How's she doing by the way?" I smirked, completely unashamed with my bisexuality while also loving how uncomfortable it made him.

Grant scoffed. "Nice, Bri. Real professional." He flipped me off and walked away, and I tried and failed to focus back on the evening I'd be having with Harrison when we got home.

With my arousal dampened, I was able to get a solid twenty minutes of actual work done. I was so focused I lost track of time, and when I remembered where I had to be, I jumped up and rushed over to the elevator. Getting in this time was harder, but knowing Harrison was in his office waiting for me gave me the push I needed to get inside.

Come on, elevator. Be nice and get me to him in the next two minutes or I'll be late.

Luckily for me, it played nice and I was rushing into his office and locking the door behind me with five seconds to spare. "Hi."

"Just in time." He stepped in behind me and tugged my skirt up above my ass. "No panties, Bri? Beautiful little slut. Were you wet for me down there in your office?"

"Fuck yes," I gasped, opening my legs and reaching out to brace against the door. "Been thinking about you all day. Been so wet for you, Sir."

"Good. You know the rules, kitten. Don't come." He knelt behind me, gripping my ass to spread my cheeks and lick my pussy, making my fingers curl painfully when my nails had nothing to hold onto.

The fact that this had been a fantasy of mine for years wasn't lost on me, and knowing I wasn't allowed to come made it even harder not to. Harrison Stag was on his knees behind me and I wasn't allowed to make a noise … it was fucking exhilarating. "S-Sir," I gasped a few moments later, after a particularly expert swipe of his tongue. "Gonna kill me, let me suck you, please."

He pulled back abruptly. "Get under my desk. You can touch yourself while you taste me, and then I'll give you a break until after work."

I barely had time to turn around before he was on his feet and fixing his suit jacket on his way to his chair, and I wasn't sure what came over me, but I dropped to my knees and crawled over to him. "Yes, Sir."

"Fucking hell, kitten." He gripped his crotch, waiting until I was right in front of him to let go. "Do you have any idea how good you look on your knees like that? Take my cock out. I'm edging for you too today, so just the tip."

I reached up to take him out, only slightly disappointed at the fact that I couldn't make him come, but I knew I'd get it before the night was over. He knew how much that meant to me. I went up on my knees more to suck in the tip, letting my eyes flutter closed as I suckled and allowed my body to relax.

"So beautiful, Briella. Love the way your mouth feels … touch your pussy for me."

I vibrated his cock with my moan the second my fingers touched my clit. It was so swollen and angry I had to move in slow, gentle circles to ensure I wouldn't come, and the way he gripped my hair and tugged only made it worse.

"My good little slut. Always happier with a cock in your mouth, aren't you?" he growled. "More. Take more."

I sucked him in deeper happily, this time making my hips twitch and grind against my hand like my cunt had a mind of its own. It made me whimper and still, reeling myself in from almost losing complete control.

"Stop," he breathed, pulling me off and squeezing the base of his cock. "Two more, kitten. One before we leave and one the minute you get to my house tonight."

I nodded, staring up into his eyes as I caught my breath. "Two more … I want to come with you inside me."

"Good choice. Now come here." He held open his arms as I climbed into his lap and let him kiss me, let his lips and tongue put me back together.

It was torture leaving him, torture trying to work until his next call came, and torture to see him walk into my office instead of making me go back up to his.

"Here." He reached into the inside pocket of his black suit jacket and pulled out one of the wearable vibes we'd bought the day after we filled out our checklists. "Put it in, kitten."

"Yes, Sir." I moved around my desk to grab it, but in one quick movement he was lifting my skirt and setting me on top of it. He guided my hand as I slipped it inside of me and then awaited more torture. "Did you already download the app?"

"Yes." He let me go only to prove it, and the moment I felt it kick to life inside of me, he yanked me to the edge of my desk and wrapped his arms around me. His thighs, those muscular, powerful thighs kept my legs spread apart so I couldn't clench, couldn't do anything but take it and bite back the moans threatening to escape.

"Oh, fuck," I whispered, my eyes dropping to the door Harrison forgot to lock. "Sir!"

"Hold on tight, kitten. I can hear it vibrating inside of you … does it feel good? Is it touching you in all the right places, making you soak the records you were proofing?" He flicked his tongue over my earlobe. "Bet that'll be hard for my beautiful little slut to explain, won't it?"

"Yes, fuck. God, it feels so good!" I lost my battle and moaned, my head falling back in pleasure as I started grinding. "I want you to fuck me so hard. Dying for your cock."

I felt the way his fingers dug into my back and hip like he was dying too, heard the growl he let out, died for the bulge rutting against me. "I will, kitten. Tonight, you're mine. You'll finally see what I can do when I'm not holding back."

He turned the intensity all the way up on that vibe until I screamed, then shut it off entirely and stepped back. In two quick movements, he had me on my feet and my skirt fixed, just in time for someone to knock on the door.

"Tell them you saw a spider," he whispered. "Now, Briella."

"Yes, I—" My voice was shaking before I cleared it. "I saw a spider. It's dead now."

Whoever it was moved on, and Harrison kissed across my jaw to my cheeks and lips. "Good girl." He put me back on my desk long enough to remove the vibe, then sucked it clean with a low moan before tucking it back into his pocket. "Straight to my house after work. I'll edge you one more time with my tongue, then give you what you want."

"Can't wait. Will you breed me again, Sir?" I reached out for him, craving his touch more with each time he edged me.

"Yes," he said honestly, sliding his hand just under my shirt to touch my skin. "Breathe for me now, kitten. Tell me one thing you love about yourself."

I knew he was just checking my headspace, so I focused on his question for a moment before I answered. "I like how dedicated I am to the things that are important to me."

"That's my good girl. Now finish your work and I'll see you later, hm? We're almost there."

I nodded and stood a little taller. "Straight to your house, go easy on them up there. I know how you are when you're pent up."

He nipped my chin with a satisfied hum. "That's half the point. I have court in an hour, and I'm not in the losing mood. I'll see you later, beautiful."

That turned me on more than I'd ever admit, and when he left my office, I slumped against my desk.

Just a few more hours.

~

Walking up to his house was even more difficult than the last time. My legs felt weak and shaky until I was naked and collapsing onto his bed, and when he walked in I thought my skin was on fire. "Sir…"

"There she is," he crooned. "My gorgeous little fucktoy. How badly do you need me, kitten?"

"So bad I'm already dripping. Want you to use me, baby. Use me and bruise me."

He looked so fucking gorgeous with his five o'clock shadow and loosened tie I wanted him to take me apart right then and there, but I knew he was far too patient for that.

No, he made me watch as he stripped slowly, folding every piece of clothing he took off. I had to lay there, stone still, as he stroked himself looking at my body and climbed up between my legs, and the command not to come yet was clear as he spit on my cunt and licked it back up.

"Fucking hell," I gasped, arching once again to chase his tongue. "It's yours."

"I know." He took me apart until I was shaking and begging him to fuck me, then rolled me over and pushed me into the mattress as he shoved my legs together and lined the tip of his cock up. "You did it, kitten. You made it through today … now come for me."

I cried out in relief as he pushed inside of me, and even louder when he gripped my wrists from behind and started pounding into me. It was everything I needed and more, everything I'd been missing in my life, and I let my eyes roll and enjoyed the ride.

"Hear how fucking wet you are? God, you were dying for my cock, huh?" He snapped his hips harder, pulling me back with each thrust until I couldn't breathe anymore.

"Sir!" I yelled, seconds before I came all over his cock and dug my nails into his wrist. It felt like my orgasm would never end, not when he praised me for squeezing him so tight, when he shifted to lean forward and fuck me into the mattress, when he whispered in my ear that he was going to claim me.

My thoughts were as erratic as my heartbeat, stopping me from asking what that meant until he spilled inside of me and held there, making sure not a drop leaked out.

"You're mine, Briella Lewis. All mine."

I was his, and with how good he was to me these days, he wouldn't hear a single complaint from me.

I couldn't wait to see what we'd do next.

Forced Orgasms

"Are you ready?" Harrison asked, his voice deep and husky in my ear.

Today was forced orgasms, something I'd never actually tried, and to say I was nervous again would be redundant. I was, but I was also so excited that those feelings of doubt were muted. "I'm ready, Sir. My body is yours."

"Good." He traced his fingers down my side and over my exposed stomach, stopping just shy of where I wanted him. "And you're still on board with the endgame we discussed, right? I make my good girl come until she falls asleep then breed her sleeping body?"

"Fuck yes," I gasped, because that question had no right being so hot. "Breed her deep please."

He rolled me onto my stomach and dragged his tongue down my spine as he spread me open. "Then don't hold back. Show me what you look like when you're sated and weak, kitten. I want it all."

His tongue, that *tongue,* danced over my ass and down to my pussy, sliding inside me as he propped my hips up to give himself better access.

I tugged on his sheets, desperate to hold onto anything sound to keep from floating away. I felt completely at his mercy, completely open and exposed, and it was amazing. "Sir!" I moaned, shuddering as his tongue took me apart at the seams, and he didn't let up for a second until I was tipping over for the first time.

"Good girl," he growled, dropping me back to my stomach and sliding two fingers inside of me. "Again."

"Yes, Sir. Fuck!" I pushed back onto his thick, skillful fingers and then rolled my hips. "I love your cock, but even your fingers feel so damn good."

"You'll get that soon," he promised, curling his fingers and biting my upper thigh. "Or maybe we'll just use your dildo."

My body twitched in pleasure as I felt myself nearing that glorious edge once again. "Please … has your slut been a good girl?"

"Let me see." He left me empty for a moment as he sucked his fingers, something I only got a chance to hear. "Yes," he muttered, spanking me twice and fingering me again. "Always so wet for me, Briella. How many years did you hide this from me? How many times did the sight of me make you wet? Did you know then that one day you'd be little more than a doll used for my pleasure?"

"Fucking shit!" I came, groaning loud with my release as I clenched around his thick digits. "Yes, Sir. Always wet for you, wanted you all over our office."

He hummed, curling his fingers and sliding them out to force them into my mouth. "Suck, Briella. Taste yourself, let me feel your tongue."

I sucked them like they were his cock, drool dripping down my chin as he moved them in and out of my mouth, and I was so close to begging for his cock it was painful.

"Good girl. My beautiful Briella … my perfect little slut. Tell me your color and one thing you love about yourself."

"Green," I cried, attempting to suck his fingers right back in but I knew him, and he wouldn't let this go until I checked in, so I blurted out the first thing I could think of. "I love my hair."

"I don't blame you, it's gorgeous." He leaned down to kiss me, then smiled almost devilishly as he pulled his cock out. "All fours, kitten. You want fucked like a whore, I'll fuck you like a whore."

"I do, Sir. I'm your dirty little whore." I got on my hands and knees and wiggled my ass at him, earning me a sharp slap then five peppered kisses over my skin.

"Say it again."

He shoved inside of me, bottoming out in one move, and his thrusts were so sharp and rough that talking at all was almost impossible.

"I'm y-your dirty little whore, all yours to use a— oh, fuck, that feels so good!" I let my face fall against the mattress as he took what he needed from me, and he dragged not one but two orgasms out of me before pulling my knees out from under me and fucking me into the mattress.

"So fucking wet for me, kitten. Never want to leave this pussy." He wrapped a hand around my throat and squeezed, forcing my back to arch and the blood flow to my head to slow, and the way his hips stung my skin as he hammered into me and bred me had me mumbling incoherent thank you's.

I was a goner … and he wasn't done with me yet.

I tensed as my dildo slid inside of my abused cunt, but the sound of him using his spend as lube had my body fully on board.

"Do you hear that, Briella? Do you hear my come? My little slut loves it, doesn't she? Such a good girl, so needy to be filled up."

I wasn't in any place to argue. I'd never been used so crudely before and I was already addicted to it. He fucked me with my dildo until I was squirting all over it, but it was obvious he still wasn't done. The second it left my body, I turned in time to see him suctioning it to the floor, and then I was being lifted and carried over to it.

Sliding down on it made me moan, and I instantly locked eyes with him and started to move. "It'll never compare to your cock, Sir."

"I know that. Don't stop, kitten. Ride it like you'd ride me. I want you to come all over it then lick it clean while you take my cock again."

Following his directions was easy even though my muscles were screaming. I trusted him more than I ever thought possible.

When I came, I allowed my eyes to close and I rode those delicious waves until my legs couldn't move any more. I pulled off with a whimper, moving around to suck that still-suctioned dildo, and the second it was in my throat Harrison's cock was pushing back inside of me. I felt so full, so used, and that alone had me coming again with a choked-off sob.

He fucked me brutally until I couldn't take it anymore, tears blurring my vision, and I was so out of it I hardly registered myself slumping against the floor.

"Good girl. You did so good, sweetheart. Look at you ... come here." He kissed me and lifted me up, then cleaned me and gave me some water before finally laying me down. With his strong arms around me, I felt myself drift off almost instantly into a dreamless sleep. All of me knew I was safe, Harrison would make sure of it.

Harrison

She was everything I'd dreamed she'd be and more. I carefully pulled off her glasses and rolled her sleeping, gorgeous body onto her side, then took my time just touching her. As much as I craved having her awake and responding to me, something about having her completely pliant and helpless underneath me turned me on to an almost concerning level — and I'd been surprised to know that somnophilia was so high on both of our lists.

She loved the idea of me using her like this as much as I did.

Slowly, I touched her hips, her sides, the smooth skin on her pussy,

admiring every inch of her body.
"So beautiful, Briella," I whispered,
carefully lifting one of her legs to
push it forward. It gave me just
enough space to line my aching
cock up and slide back into her, and
this time, I was gentle. I didn't want
to wake her, not yet. I wanted her to
wake up on her own with my come
dripping down her thighs and re-
minding her that she belonged to
me, that she was *mine,* and to know
that she couldn't escape me even in
sleep.

Over and over, I eased in and
dragged my cock back slowly as I
bent to kiss her skin. I teased her
nipples with my teeth and flicked
my tongue across her bottom lip,
and even in her sleep, she opened
for me. That single, small act of
complete submission had me snap-
ping — I licked into her mouth and
held her chin as I fucked her faster,

and I couldn't breathe as I spilled inside her pliant, limp body.

Part of me thought she woke up during that and simply didn't tell me, and most of me hoped she hadn't — but either way, as I laid down behind her and fingered my come a little deeper inside of her, I whispered praises in her ear just in case.

"So perfect for me, kitten. So worth the wait … and when you wake up, I'm going to spoil you. A bubble bath, food, a massage … you've earned it all and then some. My beautiful little Bri. I'll never get enough."

I'll never … ever get enough.

Slapping, Bondage, and Impact Play

Today was going to be huge. It had been a week since our last play session, and after an extensive discussion on what we were going to do, I couldn't have been more excited. Harrison was turning out to be an even better Dom than I ever could have imagined. He gave me exactly what I needed when I needed it, and I hadn't dropped once in his presence. The aftercare he provided was something people like me only dreamed about, and I was excited to take this next huge step.

Bondage.

When I walked into his house, he handed me a glass of water, and ever the businessman, he got right down to discussing what we were about to do for the third time.

"Are you ready?" he asked, nodding to the glass to prompt me to drink a little more.

"I'm ready for this, Sir. I really do trust you."

"Good girl. Then stretch for me. Arms and legs, then strip completely and choose your flogger."

How did I forget about that part? My whole body shivered at his command as I stripped off my clothes, and then I dropped down to stretch my legs before my arms. "Like this, Sir?"

I knew seeing me stripping naked would kill him, and I wasn't disappointed as I watched the bulge grow in his light grey sweats. "Yes, sweet-heart. Just like that. Make sure you're nice and loose. I might have you tied up for a while and I don't want you to hurt yourself."

"Promise?" I whispered, spread-ing my legs to show him how flexi-ble I truly was.

He chuckled quietly. "Which part? That I don't want you to hurt yourself, or that I'm going to keep you chained to my ceiling for hours?"

"The second part. I love pushing myself for you, Sir. I'm a lot stronger than I ever thought I was."

"You are," he confirmed, reach-ing up to touch the leather cuffs hanging from the ceiling. "Tell me your safe word and two things you love about yourself."

"Blizzard. I love my newly found strength and how flexible I am … I also love you in those sweatpants." I stood up to stretch my arms and kept my eyes on him, soaking in the way he watched me like I was something precious.

"Good girl. You're gorgeous, Briella. Will you leave your glasses on for me?"

I nodded. "If they start fogging up, can you take them off for me?"

"Of course." Harrison nodded, stepping in to help me stretch a little further. "That's my girl. Are you ready?"

"Yes, Sir. Do you want me to keep my hair down or tie it up?" I melted into him and went on my toes to inhale his neck, relaxing into his strong arms while I still could.

"Down is fine, however you're comfortable. But it's time, kitten. Pick your flogger and I'll get the spreader."

"God, that sounds so hot." I bit my lip and made my way over to his collections, sliding my fingers along the tails of a black leather flogger before grabbing it by its basket-weaved handle. "This one. Does it hurt? I've never used one with this many tresses. Just a Cat, once."

He studied me for a moment. "Try it out on yourself. Show me how my good little slut likes to be flogged."

With a soft grin, I braced one hand on the wall and brought it down on my thigh. It stung, but not nearly as bad as a whip did, and I knew I would be able to handle it for a good length of time. I did it again on my other one, this time moaning and relishing in the pain as I imagined myself completely at Harrison's mercy. "Please, Sir. I'm ready."

"Kiss me first." He took the flogger from me and wrapped one arm around my bare waist, pulling me in and kissing me fully as he backed me under those chains. I knew, whether he ever said it or not, that he valued my touch as much as I valued his — so I slid my hands all along his bare torso and gave that kiss my full attention until he had his fill.

My heart started to pound in my chest as he took my hands and brought them above my head, and he didn't break that kiss for a second as he secured my wrists in the leather cuffs. Only then did he step back to grab the ankle cuffs and the spreader bar, and he checked on me every step of the way as he spread my legs apart and clasped the bar between the cuffs.

"Comfortable, sweetheart? Do you have enough give up there?"

I tugged on it to be sure before answering. "Yes, Sir. It's perfect. Thank you."

I'd never felt more on display in my entire life, but the blindfold he wrapped around me helped. It was just me, the darkness, the cool air coming through the vent not far from me … and Harrison's hands exploring my body.

"Beautiful little doll," he whispered, slapping the inside of my thigh. "I want you to see yourself like I do. So listen closely, Briella. I'm going to tell you what I see."

I huffed and nodded quickly, letting out a low moan as he slapped my other thigh. "Yes, Sir. I'm listening."

"I see goosebumps rising over perfect skin," he muttered, slapping my stomach a little lighter. "I see a gorgeous little slut, desperate to please me."

His palm found my ass, my breasts, my hip.

"I see flushed skin just warming up for what you really need. I see straining muscles and—" teeth grazed my nipple right before he started sucking, and I barely had time to get used to the sensation before he slapped my soaked pussy and made me moan — "a pulse point I want to sink my fucking teeth into. I see a responsive, perfectly submissive, gorgeous, beautiful little slave."

Each word was accentuated by another slap, another jolt of pleasure that had my knees weak.

"Does my gorgeous little whore want it here?" he asked, lightly grazing my cheek, and I nodded quickly with a sharp breath.

"Yes, Sir. Please!"

He smacked me, hard enough to make me try to clench my thighs even though I couldn't. I knew the evidence of my arousal, of how much I fucking *loved* this was running down my thighs, and he did too when he slapped my cunt again.

"I see something that's *mine,*" he continued. "Mine to break, mine to fix, mine to love. Mine to bruise and kiss and praise and degrade and own."

The faint scraping sound of him picking up that flogger reached my ears just in time to brace myself, but the first crack had my body bowing and a whimper escaping my lips.

"Harder, Sir! Please!"

He struck me again.

"I see the marks on your skin, branding you as mine," he growled, rubbing my heated ass before dragging that flogger up between my legs to tickle my pussy.

"All of me is yours, Sir." I was surprised not being able to see him didn't dampen my tether to him. If anything, it heightened it. His arousal was palpable, I didn't need to see how much he was tenting and leaking in those sweats, I could fucking feel it.

"And all of me is yours, Briella." He dropped that flogger, sliding two fingers inside of me as he wrapped his arm around my waist from behind and kissed my shoulder. "Let go for me, gorgeous. Be my good girl and give it to me."

"Oh, thank fuck!" I gasped, my head falling back and exposing my neck for him. "I'm gonna come. Fuck, that feels so goddamn good!"

He kissed all over my neck, shoulder, my raised arm, driving his fingers into me faster and pulling back at the exact moment to make me squirt.

And with as badly as I craved his cock, I was completely caught off guard with how amazing it felt. I heard the splash of it hit his wood floor, felt my body convulse as more gushed out and then I finally found my words. "T-thank you, Sir."

Expert hands untied my wrist cuffs, then helped steady me before that blindfold was removed and he knelt down to free my legs. A moment later, he swept me up to carry me to the bed.

"You know my rules, kitten. I'm going to kiss every spot I slapped five times while you tell me five things you love about yourself. Begin."

My back hit the soft mattress as his lips danced over my skin, making my mind slowly come back to me as each kiss grounded me back on Earth. "I—" I took a breath and started again. "I love my mind, my ability to fight through anything, my … strong pain tolerance. Um, my adaptability. Is that five, Sir? Does the one earlier count?"

"It can count." He kissed his way all the way up my body to my cheek and then my lips, and that slow, sweet kiss nearly made me cry. "Next time, we'll use the flogger a little more. You did incredible for your first time, kitten … but now I need you to come with me. I need to check the impact spots so I can treat them if necessary."

I nodded, letting him lift me up and carry me to his well-lit bathroom, and watching him care for me and dote on me felt better than almost everything else.

Almost.

Voyeurism

Breathe, I reminded myself, but it was easier said than done.

I was on my knees between Harrison's legs, him fully clothed in a delicious, navy-blue suit, me completely naked aside from my glasses and the purple vibrator he was currently holding against my clit. We were watching the hottest threesome I'd ever seen, one man sitting on a couch, a beautiful blonde spearing herself on his fat cock with another man in her mouth. I could have come just from watching her get used, but seeing as I hadn't been given permission yet, I was hanging on by a thread.

"Beautiful, aren't they? Can you imagine how many times she's taken their cocks like this, and now she's doing it just for you?" Harrison whispered, lightening the pressure a little bit. "Bet my good girl would take them even better, but we'll never know."

"No?" I asked, unable to help myself. "Why not, Sir?"

His free hand wrapped around my neck and his voice dropped. "Because you're mine, kitten. I told you in that elevator that no one would ever touch you again, and I meant it," he growled. "Are you telling me you want them?"

"No," I rushed out. "Not even a little bit, I wanted to hear you s-say that." I couldn't lie to him, not even if it meant I might be punished.

JENSEN

"Good. You should be grateful that I even agreed to let you be this close. They can see you, you know. See your legs splayed and your pretty little mouth hanging open. Derek offered me money to be able to fuck your throat, did you know that?" he asked, upping the intensity on that vibrator and pressing it a little harder against me. "He wanted to buy you, said that's what whores are for."

I moaned, body twitching with the need for release at his words. "Sir," I gasped. "What would you do if he tried?"

"I don't think you want me to answer that."

The malice and promise in his voice had me nearly coming without permission, but I held off and dug my nails into my thighs. It also helped when I watched the man pull his cock out and slap her with it, but

55

then he moved behind her to slide in her ass. It was so fucking hot I lost my breath. "Sir, Sir I'm close."

"Then beg, kitten. Beg louder than Ashlyn is moaning and maybe I'll let you come." He sucked a mark on my neck as he tapped my clit with the vibrator, making my thighs shake and begging nearly impossible, but I managed to find my voice after a moment.

"Please! Please let me come, I'll be your good girl."

"I know you will, perfect girl. Come for me."

He dropped the toy and hooked two fingers inside of me, giving me exactly what I needed to come with a choked-off groan, making the three putting on a show turn to watch. It was exhilarating … and I could tell I wasn't done. "Thank you, Sir."

"You're welcome, kitten. Now do it again," he commanded, shifting me so I was sitting on my ass with my legs spread, and he put that vibrator back to my throbbing clit. "Tell Derek and Gabriel what you want them to do to her."

Both men turned to look at me as Ashlyn tried to catch her breath, and the power I felt radiating through my body had my confidence booming. "Keep making her scream. She's so fucking hot when she screams, but don't let her finish. Not until her face is painted with both of your come."

Harrison started tapping my clit again as Derek slid back in Ashlyn's ass and Gabriel started fucking her throat, and it didn't take him long to pull back and coat her cheeks as Derek fucked her harder.

She got so loud and desperate that I almost took pity on her —

but Harrison's voice in my ear had me distracted. "The scent of you is driving me insane, kitten. My hand is soaked and I can smell you from up here … you're going to make me ruin my suit."

"God, I hope you do. I'm so fucking close again, I—" I moaned right along with Ashlyn as Derek pulled out of her ass and moved to come all over her face, and seeing her that way had me following her instantly.

With Gabriel's fingers inside of Ashlyn now, we got off together, filling the space with desperate moans and the sinful sound of how wet we really were.

"Good girl," Harrison growled, kissing over my shoulder as he finally let me rest. "So beautiful, Briella."

"Thank you, Sir. Can I suck you?" I asked, my eyes fluttering closed as I let the exhaustion take over my body. But even this drained, I wanted to please him.

"Will you stay awake long enough after to get cleaned up and drink your water?" he asked.

"Mmhm," I hummed. "Promise. But first, I want you to use my throat. Show me I was a good girl."

He glanced up to the others. "Out. Make sure Ashlyn gets the aftercare she needs or I'll knock you both out."

Gabriel carried her as Harrison let me turn around and nodded to his crotch, telling me silently to take him out.

With my bottom lip between my teeth I reached up to slowly unzip his zipper, never breaking eye contact no matter how badly I wanted to watch that gorgeous cock spring free.

"Tell me two things you love about yourself and then suck me, kitten."

The fucking restraint it must have taken him to do this first had me purring and clinging to his slacks. No matter the situation, he always put me first. "I love my pussy, and how much it loves pleasing you, and I love my breasts." I cupped them and squeezed, then slowly leaned forward to suck him in and stop more words from falling from my lips, because I nearly confessed my love for him.

"Good girl." He let go for a while, whispering praises as I sucked him, then pet my face once he was close. "Now I'm going to tell you three things I love about you, and then I'm going to come down your tight little throat. Understood?" The moment I nodded and slid him deeper, he fisted a hand in my hair and took control. "I love the way your glasses fog up when I use your throat ... I love how you're never afraid to test your boundaries, and I love the fact that you fucking belong to *me.*"

He slammed deep, making my nose sting with the impact as he pulsed and emptied down my throat, and I stayed there for a while after just breathing with him. He saw me for who I was, he saw me and he still wanted me, and not one part of me was complaining.

I belonged to him.

Anal/Body Worship

"That feels so good, Sir." I released a heavy breath as all the tense muscles began to truly relax. It was a long week at the office for both of us, and this was exactly the contact we needed.

His thumbs gently dug into the knots just under my shoulder blades as he hummed. "You deserve this, beautiful. My beautiful, strong Briella."

"You're going to spoil me … please don't stop." I smiled, wiggling my ass a little to rub against his crotch and test his restraint.

"You can't tempt me, devil woman. In a few short hours, I'll have an entire day with this ass to myself. For now, I just want you to relax. You're safe here with me and your phone is off, which means none of my idiotic coworkers will be calling you for late-night favors. Just breathe for me, Briella."

I had to admit, it felt fucking amazing. I'd been craving him for a couple days, craving his cock as much as his gorgeous hands and knowing he was doing this just for me had me fully relaxing. I let my eyes close to breathe with him, focusing on nothing but the way his hands made my tension disappear. He was speaking, I knew he was, but for once … I wasn't listening.

At least not until he called my name twice. "Bri?"

"Hmm?" I hummed quickly, jerking slightly in surprise. "Yes, Sir? I'm here."

"How many times did you come today?"

"The two times you allowed, Sir. I'd never come without your permission." I moved a little again, wanting to see his face but he was still on top of me.

He gently held me down and clicked his tongue to tell me to stay. "That wasn't why I was asking, kitten. Did you drink your water?"

I stayed put, even though the click of his tongue did things to me. "Yes, Sir. All sixteen ounces. Have you come today?"

"Once. And yes, I drank my eight ounces too," he muttered playfully. "Now relax, you can sleep as long as you need to. Prep yourself in the morning when you're ready and come find me. I'll be in my office."

JENSEN

He rubbed a little lower, and I
closed my eyes to listen. I wanted
him, wanted so much more, but my
Sir knew what I needed and I was in
no place to argue. Tomorrow would
be perfect.

~

In the morning after breakfast, I
did exactly as I was told. I showered
and cleaned myself out well,
prepped my ass with the toys he laid
out for me, and when I was ready to
go to him, I slipped on a silk robe
and left a plug inside me.

I found him in his office like he
said, looking like a whole damn
meal in his sweats, and it made me
wish he could wear those to work
sometimes. The second that thought
crossed my mind, I dismissed it, because something about this being

just for my eyes made me feel special. "Good morning, Sir."

"Kitten." He eyed me, slowly tilting his laptop screen down to get a better look at me. "Did you sleep well?"

"Of course. I always do when I stay here with you. Did you?" I moved closer, running a finger down the flaps of my robe toward the tie.

He nodded once, sliding his chair back a little. "I sleep better when you're here, too. Come here, sweetheart."

I kept my agonizingly slow pace as I untied my gown and let it fall to the floor, then straddled his thigh with my eyes locked on his.

"Every inch of you was made for me," he whispered, leaning in to kiss my bare skin as his arms wrapped around me. "My infuriating, stubborn, incredible Briella."

I let my head fall back with a gasp, hoping that he always felt that way about me. "Yours."

I rubbed my clit along his thigh with a moan as his teeth caught my nipple, but he only let me stay like that a moment before lifting me up and carrying me downstairs.

The bed was already covered in plush, dark grey towels, there was water and lube on the nightstand, and the floodlights down there were turned a deep, crimson red.

"Don't take this personal, kitten, but I'm not planning on coming until you're begging me to stop touching you."

"Yes, Sir." My skin began to buzz in a way I'd linked to him, only him. "Lights feel familiar." Suddenly I was back in that hell of an elevator and I couldn't breathe, but it wasn't air that I craved. It was him. "Please touch me."

He took his time, kissing every inch of my body and whispering praises against my skin until I was arching to chase his lips. Only then did he flip me, spanking me lightly and kissing the spot as he toyed with that plug.

"How does it feel?"

That spank had my attention firmly back on him — the him in that moment, not the him I once thought hated me before the earthquake. "Feels good, Sir. Just not as good as your fingers do."

"You'll get them soon." He kissed over my ass and swirled his tongue around the flared rim of the plug filling me up, and I fought the painful urge to move and grind against his face.

"Oh god," I breathed, shuddering when he did it again.

"Stay still, kitten. I'm going to take it out, okay?" The moment I said yes, he eased it out of me and tossed it on the floor, then palmed my ass to spread me open. "Does my beautiful little slut want more?"

"Yes," I moaned. "Please, Sir. More." He dove back in, swirling his tongue along the entrance with his fingers digging into my skin. He ate my ass for so long it started to feel numb where his hands were, and when I couldn't take it anymore I whimpered. "S-sir, please. Please I need more, need your fingers."

He pulled back, slapping my ass twice before grabbing the lube and coating his fingers. "How many, kitten? You choose."

"Three," I begged. "Three of them, please. One more spanking?"

This time, he brought his hand up harder and made my ass shake, then slid three fingers inside of me. "My beautiful Briella wants her ass stuffed full, hm?"

"Yes, Sir!" I groaned, pushing back on his fingers and relishing the burn. I'd always loved pain, I thought back to the times that I'd spank my thighs with my own belt before I touched myself and moaned again. "So fucking good. Again, please."

Over and over, he alternated spanking me and fingering me until I was so desperate to feel his cock I couldn't stand it. "Beg, Briella. I can feel you're there, so beg me."

"Pl-ease!" My body began to tremble as it floated somewhere between pain and pleasure, and for me, those lines had always been intertwined. "I need your cock."

"Good girl. Come here."

Harrison sat back, pulling me onto his lap and holding my back to his chest as he eased inside me. Steadily, he rolled his hips and slapped my pussy, tugging my thighs further apart until I was spread out and speared on his cock. "How sore are you, beautiful?"

"Feels like you're stretching me further than ever before, it's so sore. I love it." My hand flew back to grip his hair, which only made those thrusts sharper, harder, faster.

"So fucking tight, Bri," he gasped. "Fucking strangling my cock. Clench for me … pull harder."

Knowing he was coming apart just like I was felt amazing, like maybe he was feeling exactly how I was feeling about all of it and maybe we were completely on the same page. I clenched as tightly as I could, tugging harder on his hair with a jerk.

His fingers rubbed my clit faster, slapping down every few seconds as he rolled his hips and feverishly kissed my neck. "Come, Briella.

Come for me so I can take you apart."

"Yes, yes, I'm coming." The air left my lungs once again, and this time, it had me squirting all over his hand.

I *heard* him snap behind me.

My face hit the pillow as he flipped me forward and slipped out, then shoved back inside my sore, abused ass and fucked me into the mattress. I was screaming — screaming for more, for him to stop, for him to keep going until I cried — but for the first time, the great Harrison Stag found his limit before I found mine.

"God damnit, Briella!" He came with a grunt, fucking it deeper and pinning me down by the back of my neck as he spanked me so hard I cried out in pain.

"Sir," I pleaded, but for what, I wasn't sure. "Sir …"

He eased out carefully and flipped me over again and tucking his arm under me to hold me. "You were incredible, Bri. Better than … fuck. You're my best girl, my beautiful Bri."

The praise kept me grounded, kept my thin, transparent tether to him strong. "Thank you, Sir. I can feel your come … it's so deep inside me."

"Of course it is, because you take me so well. Can you stand? I desperately want to kiss you but given where I've had my mouth recently …" He smirked as he backed up and helped me to the edge of the bed, making me stand on wobbly, unsure knees.

"My legs feel heavy," I muttered, and when he scooped me up off my feet, I was back in that elevator once again — only this time, it was the memory of him carrying me to safety. "Thank you," I repeated, meaning it for so much more than just sex.

And somehow, I knew he knew it.

Check In/ Exhibitionism

Harrison

I let my mind wander as I cleaned up the dishes from the dinner we shared. We'd come so far in such a short time — I knew she trusted me, and beyond that, I trusted myself with her. What she was giving me was something precious.

And I wasn't about to take it for granted.

"So," I said, sitting back down and sliding her a glass of her favorite wine. "Time for another one of those conversations that make you blush so beautifully. I know we've touched base before, during, and after every scene, but I'd like to talk about them now that you've had some time to … digest."

She took a long sip as she eyed me over the glass and considered her words. "Okay. Yeah, that's probably a good thing. Thanks for … y'know, helping me communicate."

"Thank you for following the rules," I countered. "Now, is there anything you'd like to say? Things you enjoyed, things you need but aren't getting from me, things that you don't necessarily want to try again?"

I appreciated the amount of thought she gave it before responding. "You're doing more than I ever expected or have experienced in my life. Because of that, it's easy to enjoy everything with you so far. You cause the perfect amount of pain and care, I — I can't think of anything I wanted done differently, but I will continue to think about that if it ever does happen."

"Thank you." I took a moment to watch her, to take in the way she chewed her bottom lip. "Are you sure you're up for what we're doing next?"

In watching her, I didn't miss the tiniest upturn of those lips. "Yes. Will I be punished for being excited?"

"No. I'm not going to punish you for enjoying yourself, Briella ... especially since we're only doing this for you. Do you think I'm excited to watch other men come-mark you?" I muttered. "This was quite a loophole you found, and I suppose I can blame that on your career choice."

She looked far too proud of herself. "I'm still yours. All of me, Sir."

"I know. And I'm reserving the right to throat punch anyone that disobeys me during this. If either of them so much as brush the hair out of your face, you're going to witness a massacre." I let out a slow breath but kept her pinned with my gaze, hoping she understood how thoroughly I meant that in a hypothetical sense. "And if you touch one of them …"

"I won't. I don't want to touch anyone but you, Harrison. I want to touch you all the time … even at work when you have your angry face on."

I wanted to pretend I didn't know what she was talking about, but even in that moment, I could *feel* it — my brows were pinched, lips turned down, eyes narrowed. Even the thought of others watching her again was making my blood boil. "I'm glad you feel that way, kitten, because they'll be watching me breed you before any of them are allowed to come anywhere near you." I paused. "Pun intended."

She huffed, then finished her wine and moved over to straddle me. "Puns are less funny when you look mad, you know." Her fingers curled into the front of my shirt as she gazed into my eyes. "I love it when you breed me … when you claim me as yours."

Then why am I not enough? I took a deep, slow breath as I touched her hips, and reminded myself that this was a process. We'd spent a decade at each other's throats, punishing each other for the attraction we were only now beginning to explore, and there were things about her that I couldn't bring myself to make her give up. "So kiss me, then go upstairs and wait for me in the shower. Be prepared to take two today, by the way. Once now and once the moment they leave. I'll clean you myself both times. Is that alright?"

"Absolutely. Thank you, Sir. You take such good care of me." Briella kissed me much deeper than I expected before she went on her way, and I tipped my head back the moment she was out of sight.

I can do this for her, I can be this for her. Thou shall not kill, thou shall not gouge someone's eyes out for looking at her, thou shall not ... fuck it. I'll do what the moment demands.

We ended up being late joining the others downstairs since I couldn't bring myself to stop touching her in that shower, and by the time I was nodding to Derek, Gabriel, and Ryan, I was ready to ruin her.

"You're all aware of the ground rules, yes?"

"Absolutely, Boss. No touching," Derek confirmed, but I didn't miss

80

the way he was already looking at her and how hard he was in his basketball shorts, and Ryan was no better.

"Didn't expect her to be so beautiful. Will she keep the glasses on?"

Every fucking red-blooded inch of me wanted to say no, but the whole goddamn point of this was for Briella to enjoy herself. Since she wouldn't be able to rely on touch for that, she'd need to be able to see. "Yes," I growled. "Touch each other all you like, but not her. Not Her."

Gabriel held his hands up. "Hey, we knew what we signed up for. Can we talk to her at all?"

Again, I wanted to say no, but I paced my breaths for a moment and then nodded to Bri. "I will leave that up to you. It's not my favorite idea, but I will not blame you or punish you if you say yes."

"I want them to talk *about* me but not *to* me. I want to hear all the dirty little things they'd say about the cockslut in front of them, but only you can speak directly to me."

A little part of me wanted to worship her for that, but she'd set the tone with that request. She was here to be degraded, so despite my instinct to praise her above all else, I would give her what she asked for.

"Then get on your knees, little whore. Show them exactly what they'll be missing as they're using their own hands to do what your mouth is about to do to me. Get me nice and wet."

Her gaze dropped a second before her body did, knees thumping softly against the cold, unforgiving wood, and then she slid her hands up my thighs toward my cock.

When she sucked me in, I did my best to ignore the others and just focus on her tongue. None of them mattered, and as far as I was concerned, none of them were even there — but the constant stream of "She really is a cockslut," and "Look at her take that cock like she was born for it," had me tensing.

"Is this what you wanted, beautiful?" I whispered. "Are your fingers itching to touch, to have two fat cocks in your hand while I fuck your throat?"

I felt her groan as much as I heard it, and I could see her fingers twitching against her thighs as she fought the urge to say yes. It was the talk that got to her, not the actual act, but the idea and degradation that came along with it. That's what she craved.

At least that's what I told myself.

"Bet that wouldn't be enough, huh? Not when you've got two greedy little holes between your thighs. Bet my little slut wouldn't be happy until she couldn't possibly take another one, hm?" I gripped her hair and pulled out, smacking her face with my cock. "Say it, kitten."

Briella moaned at the impact. "Yes, Sir. I'm your greedy slut."

She moved to suck me back in hungrily, and I let her go until I couldn't hold back anymore. I yanked her off and dropped to my knees, then wrapped my hands around her thighs to flip her backward on the ground. I knew they were jacking off above us, whispering to each other and fantasizing about actually touching her, touching *my* Briella, wondering if they'd get away with it if they disobeyed me and just dragged a fingertip down her skin to her wet fucking cunt and I … snapped.

"Mine," I growled, slamming deep too fast, pinning her shoulders to the cold ground as I drove myself into her body over and over again, grunting with the strain as I tried to erase them and what they were doing from my mind. There was only her, only me, only this.

And it was only *my* honorific she was moaning.

"Sir, I've been such a bad girl. Such a bad slut craving the attention of other men. They want to fuck me so bad they're shaking ... show them who I belong to."

I slapped her hard enough to sting my palm and shoved two fingers into her mouth, prying her jaw open as I fucked her harder. "They know you're mine. Three of them and one of me, they could take you if they really wanted, it's not like you'd say no ... but you're mine, kitten. My beautiful little slut, and everyone knows it." I leaned down to spit in her mouth as I hit the edge, and the way she clenched around me as she came had me emptying fully inside her — but I wasn't pulling out.

"You've got thirty seconds," I snapped to the others. "Briella, close your fucking mouth."

Gabriel and Derek both dropped down, bracing themselves on each other's shoulders as they jacked off over her body, but Ryan stayed standing. Bri arched off the ground and reached up to rub her tits.

"Fuck," she gasped, then snapped her mouth shut as Derek began to come with a long, drawn-out groan.

"Fucking slut," he growled, stroking himself until he was spent and her chin and neck were covered.

I barely registered the others covering her stomach. All I saw was red as white hot fury raged through me, and I nearly broke my own rule. "Out," I snapped. "Apologize to her for speaking to her and then get out."

"Shit, sorry. Sorry, Harrison." The fact that he thought to apologize to me might have helped if I still wasn't so fucking angry.

They rushed from the room as Briella stared into my eyes and played with the mess on her skin, and it took me several, agonizing moments to control my breathing and remember that this was for her, not me, and I'd fucking agreed to it. "Five things you ... love about yourself, Briella. Now."

"Sir ..." she whispered, her hands stopping completely as she sat up. "My hips, lips, strength, sense of humor, and my um, nipples." It was obvious she blurted those things out just for me, but then she said something that surprised the hell out of me. "Sir, can you please tell me five things you like about yourself? Please."

I met her eyes and licked my lips slowly, drawing nothing but blanks. "I'm … excellent at my job, I …" I huffed, sitting back on my knees and reaching to hand her a bottle of water. "Fuck. Give me a minute."

She drank it and handed it back for me to drink too, watching me too closely, and from one glance at her I could tell she wasn't going to let up.

"I'm excellent at my job, I'm a good brother, I'm great at managing money, I put aftercare above pleasure, and I'm a surprisingly good dog dad, though I haven't had one since my last died." I counted those back in my head then nodded, a little proud of myself. "Bring me your face, I owe your cheek five kisses for slapping you."

"Thank you, Sir." She leaned in and closed her eyes as I placed gentle kisses against her chin, then held onto her face for a proper one. "Shower with me, can I clean you too this time? It's just you and me now. Just you and me."

The fucking reminder that she was covered in other people's come had me growling without even realizing it, and I abruptly let her go when it hit me that I was digging my fingers into her hips. "Yes, that would be … good."

I scooped her up and carried her there quickly, getting us both under the water before it warmed up. I had her skin clean and her hair washed before my entire body was even wet, and only then did I relax enough to let her touch me.

"My safe word is 'Caterpillar,'" I mumbled. "I wouldn't have used it today, but that was the closest I think I've ever come to needing one."

"Thank you for sharing it with me. I was going to ask once we were in bed. I'm sorry, Sir. I love when you get territorial and possessive, I shouldn't have pushed that hard." She moved behind me and started on my back with slow, soothing circles. "I'm yours," she reminded me gently. "There's no one else for me."

I shook my head. "Don't apologize, Briella. I'm the one who said yes. The day I punish you for one of my decisions, you should run. I should've communicated more openly when we discussed this to begin with, but part of me knows my feelings aren't fair to you here. I've craved you for ten years, and I *finally* got you to myself. I think maybe we tried that too soon."

"I understand. It was very soon. We can put that experience on a shelf for now and discuss it later. I've craved you for ten years too, Harrison. And it isn't fair because I'd have slapped a hoe."

I turned to face her and kiss her deeply. "We'll do better tomorrow, and the day after that, and the day after that. And maybe one day I'll be ready to try that again, but … probably not." I smiled against her lips then held her to me under the water, loving the way her small body fit against mine. "You're beautiful, Briella. Still my good girl."

Her fingers curled against my back as she relaxed into me. "You're the best Dom I've ever heard of, and I'm including romance novels."

"I'm not, not by a long shot, but I'll take the compliment and say thank you. So ... thank you." I tipped her chin up to kiss her again and then knelt to let her finish cleaning me, and each touch helped ground me again.

Everything was going to be fine. She was still mine.

The Game

"Good morning, Harrison." I kissed his shoulder and plopped up on the counter to watch him cook breakfast. "One of these days I'll beat you in here and cook breakfast for you."

"Doubt it, but you're welcome to try." He smirked slightly as he flipped the pancakes. "Did you wake up in a competitive mood today, kitten?"

"Maybe." I bit my lip and eyed him, knowing damn well I'd never wake up first and miss out on his cooking. "What are you gonna do about it if I am?"

He hummed, licking the batter off the spoon. "Probably fuck that attitude out of you."

I couldn't stop the stupid, giddy smile that spread across my face. "How am I supposed to not want to take that challenge?"

"I didn't say you shouldn't take it." He shut the stove off and caged me on that counter. "Now we just need to pick a game."

"Hmm ... should it be sexual? Or juvenile?" I kissed his neck to sway him into the direction I wanted.

The growl he let out answered for him. "Sexual."

It was so ... easy ... to wake up the beast.

I flicked my tongue along his skin to keep him awake, then reached down to palm him. "What'd you have in mind, Harrison?"

"It's hard to concentrate with you doing that," he mumbled. "But you seem to think you've got some self-control today, am I right?"

"For sure. You thinking edging?" I kept going, kept pushing him until he slid his hand up to grip the sides of my throat.

"That's too easy. My good little slut loves to edge, so where's the challenge in that? I say you try not to come at all, and I do everything in my power to make you come until you cry."

It was a challenge I couldn't fucking wait to lose. "Game on, Mr. Stag. Let's see who's crying in the end."

"Eat your breakfast first, Briella. Maybe have a cup of coffee. As much as I love fucking you while you sleep, I want you awake for this," he said, voice thick with sinful promise. "You need to be alert to say 'uncle.'"

"What happens if you say 'uncle' first?" I challenged, hopping off the counter and moving toward the food to serve our plates.

He eyed me a little warily. "I'm not sure. You'd be the victor in that insane little scenario, so you tell me."

"I'll think about it." I put extra syrup on my pancakes and licked some off my finger. "And when do you get to come?"

"That depends," Harrison said carefully. "Who are you today, Briella? My beautiful, strong, good girl … or are you a bad little slut who deserves to be used?"

That was a tricky one. I loved being his slut he could use, but I loved being his good girl more than anything. "Can I be both? Your beautiful, strong slut?"

"You always are. I won't come until you do, deal?"

"Okay, deal. I wouldn't be able to hold off if I watched you come, so that's fair." Part of me had hoped he'd make me suffer by coming, but I knew for sure I'd lose if he did.

He tilted his head as he took a bite. "Cute that you assume coming is the only way I can break you," he mused. "I'm going to have fun taking you apart, Briella. Now eat your pancakes, and I want you to play with your clit while you do."

"Starting already?" I stripped off my clothes for him and took a seat, reaching between my legs to touch my clit as I took my next bite. "This good, Sir?

"Yes." His intense gaze never left me as we ate, and the moment we were done, he shoved every one of those plates to the floor and came around to put my ass on the table. "Are you ready?"

"Fuck yes." And I was, my clit was already so swollen I considered saying fuck the game and fuck me, but I held on strong and spread wide for him. "Ready for you."

"There's my good girl," he whispered, dancing his fingertips over my thighs, ghosting over my pussy and up my stomach. "Close your eyes."

My head fell back as I complied, knees shaking slightly as his touch left scorch marks on my skin and I forced myself to think about anything but that, but within minutes, I was failing.

Harrison didn't stop. "Keep those eyes closed, kitten. Lose yourself to how this feels, to how hard just touching your skin makes me.

Do you feel that? Feel my hard cock sliding into you?"

I didn't, but that didn't mean the words didn't make me clench.

"That's it, beautiful," he continued. "You drive me crazy when you clench like that, when all I feel is your wet cunt wrapped around me as I thrust harder, needing to be deeper inside you."

His fingers trailed lower, back to my thighs, and I thought he was finally going to give me what I needed but he kept them there, circling and teasing all the right places to keep me tense and desperate. "Sir …"

"Shh … just take it, kitten. Take my cock, just like this." He slapped my pussy so sharply it made me cry out in a mix of pleasure and pain, and I fought an overwhelming urge to lean forward and bite him. "So fucking responsive. Clench for me again, sweetheart, let me feel you squeeze my cock until I'm breeding you again. Think it'll take this time? Think this will finally be the time I *really* breed you?"

His voice, that low, wrecked voice made it easy for me to picture it, to picture him pumping me full until my belly swelled with our love and created something brand new. I nearly cried for it. "Please!"

"That's it, kitten, beg. My good little slut sounds so pretty when she begs. You want to come? Ask me fucking nicely."

I growled slightly, a small, desperate noise that came from deep inside my chest. "Please, Sir. Please fuck your come deep inside me until I carry your baby."

He had me off that table and pinned to the kitchen floor so fast it almost knocked the wind out of me, but feeling him finally slide inside of me for real was worth it. "That's a good girl," he growled. "My good little slut. Are you going to come for me now?"

"No," I gasped, not as convincing as I'd hoped. "Not going to come, Sir."

"Now you're a bad girl." He dug his fingers into my hips and held me down, grinding deep. "Maybe I won't let you come at all then."

I was going to lose.

In a matter of seconds, I wanted to take it all back and give in to the release I'd been craving, but I had to stand my ground. Caving was what he wanted. Instead, I embraced the bad girl, embraced how wound up I was making him every time I denied him, and then I slapped him.

He barely flinched, but the wicked smile that spread across his face set me on fire. "Congratulations, Briella. Change of plans. Now you're going to come for me whether you like it or not." Harder, *harder* those thrusts became as he wrapped a hand around my throat and choked me. "So fucking wet. You feel so good wrapped around me, Briella. Clenching and *so fucking wet.* Color?"

"Green!"

"Good girl. Then your choices are to come for me or pass out. I don't care which, I'll be filling you up soon either way."

The implication that he'd come inside me regardless had me hurtling toward the edge, and after the weakest grunt I could muster, my body began to shake. It was over, I'd lost … or maybe I'd won, because it was truly one of the best orgasms of my life.

I hovered somewhere between consciousness and unconsciousness, grasping onto him with a skin-piercing hold as I failed to call his name and soaked his cock.

"God, I'll never get over how fucking good that feels," he hissed breathlessly, dropping down to pin me fully as his hips lost rhythm and he let my throat go. "Thank you, Briella. Always my good girl. So f— oh, god."

He kissed me fiercely as his cock pulsed inside of me so deep I could barely breathe, and I smiled as my feet planted firmly on the "I won" side of things.

Because I did.

And he was my prize.

Punishment

"Yes, Grant, I've got it." I hung up the phone a little too forcefully and gripped my hair with both hands. Of all the long days of being a paralegal, that day was the longest.

I didn't see Harrison once, which was unusual since we started our relationship, and Grant was so far up my ass about a case I nearly called Harrison to get out of it. *No. You've never called Harrison or any upper management man to fight your battles before, you will not start that today. Breathe.* Somehow the voice in my head was suddenly Harrison's, and I took a breath, then went to our text thread to check in with him. He'd already talked me off via text three times that day, and because of those orgasms, I'd managed to not kill anyone. I needed to say thank you.

Me: *Can I see you tonight? Need to feel you breed me.*

Sir: *I have a late deposition tonight so it'll be a while, but I'll leave my key on my desk. Just come grab it and go home to wait for me.*

I slumped into my chair before responding.

Me: *Yes, Sir. I'll take care of dinner.*

Sir: *Thank you, beautiful. Are you okay?*

Me: *Yes. Long day but I know yours is just as long.*

Me: *Question for a friend. If I punched Grant, would I be fired?*

A moment later, a voice memo came through instead of a text. He said, "Thought it was better not to text this for plausible deniability, but if you're going to hit him, go to the break room down there and make sure to wrap your fist in something first so you don't break your knuckles or get blood on you. No one will know but me."

I grinned, listening to it three times before I responded.

Me: *Your voice does things to me. Thank you, I see why you're such an amazing defense attorney.*

Sir: *Does it?*

He sent another voice clip, this time of him growling quietly. "So beautiful, Briella. My good girl isn't allowed to have a bad day, so cheer up and take care of yourself until I can take care of you tonight."

Sir: *Have to run, kitten. Come get the key, it's under the "Worst Lawyer Ever" mug you got me in the secret Santa exchange a few years ago.*

I chuckled, genuinely surprised he still had it.

Me: *I don't know why you assumed that was from me, but it was. :) See you later, Sir.*

I felt better just hearing from him and instantly started packing up my things. The witness' paperwork he dropped on my desk could wait, Grant could wait. I was already setting my own work on the back burner for him as it was, I wasn't going to let him ruin my evening any longer.

Before I left the office, I grabbed Harrison's key, left a lipstick mark on a napkin for him, then ordered us some Chinese takeout and made my way toward the elevator.

Getting on it was always a process for me.

I took my deep breaths, contemplating all those stairs as usual and convinced myself that I'd probably pass out if I tried to climb down nearly seventy floors. I was starving, and Harrison told me to take care of myself — something told me fainting would have been the opposite.

I stopped breathing entirely when it started to move, then melted into the corner in an attempt to steady my heart. I hated that fucking hell box, but changing jobs wasn't an option for me. I wouldn't leave everything I'd worked for because of some new fear for elevators ... regardless of how heavy that fear now was.

Twenty more floors.

I glanced at the place where I'd fucked Harrison for the first time and focused on that instead. Objectively, I knew this was an entirely new elevator, there was no more chandelier painting, no ridiculous mirrors reflecting fear, just a mural of San Francisco and international orange carpet to match the Golden Gate Bridge. It wasn't the place I had sex with Harrison for the first time, but my desperate need for a distraction made me think about it anyway.

It was the only way I made it every day without having a panic attack.

My legs wobbled as I made it to the bottom floor, and it wasn't until I was out of it that I inhaled a true breath of air and relaxed.

I made it.

I felt better by the time I entered Harrison's house, especially after I ate my dinner and took a shower, but by that point I was beyond ready to be in his arms.

He must've sensed how badly I needed him because he didn't make me wait long — he walked in just after nine and pulled me into a hug, kissing all over the top of my head. "I like coming home to you."

"Yeah?" Butterflies erupted inside of me, because I really fucking liked it too. "You don't mind that I used your shower and stole your shirt?" I grinned, biting my lift softly as I lifted it and showed him the *nothing* I was wearing under it.

"Not at all." He set his briefcase down and loosened his tie, then dropped to his knees and pulled me in to kiss my pussy. He playfully grabbed that shirt and pulled it over his head with a happy hum, rubbing his nose against my clit to make me laugh. "Just leave me here to die."

"That kinda day, huh?" I ran my hand along his head softly and stared down at the lump with a grin. "I missed you."

He surfaced again with a dramatic sigh. "It's always that kind of day, but it's better now. How many glasses of water have you had today?"

Fuck. The water. I panicked, eyes darting around the room as I pretended I was fine. "Um, two, I think." It wasn't enough, I knew it wasn't enough. "I can have more now." *Even though my last orgasm was hours ago.*

"And how many times have you gotten off in the last twenty-four hours?" he asked, deflating slightly.

"Three, Sir." I already missed where he was, where we would have been if I'd have followed directions. "I deserve my punishment."

"My rules are simple, Briella. One glass of water for every time you come to ensure you stay hydrated, you allow me five kisses to any spot on your gorgeous body that I slap to ensure you remember that I'll always take care of you, and degradation is paid for with praise from me and self-praise from you to ensure you stay in the right headspace and always remember how special you are. Why did you forget?" he asked, gripping my shirt and pulling me closer. "Explain."

"I was busy. I skipped a lunch too and just forgot about my health completely. I'm sorry, Sir."

He wrapped me up in another hug and kissed the top of my head. "You ate dinner, yes? Drink another glass of water for me right now and I'll keep the punishment light."

A light punishment sounded like less than I deserved, because his instructions and rules were so simple as it was, but I wasn't in any place to argue. I made my way to the kitchen for a glass of water and handed him another, then drank it in its entirety before responding. "Can I ask what it is?"

"One of the ones we've previously agreed on," he said simply. "You know how difficult it is to punish someone who loves to be spanked and edged and degraded, so I'm going to get you off and then you'll watch me come without you. But that's where it will end. We'll get cleaned up after and you'll drink your water and fall asleep in my arms like always."

I dropped my eyes to his crotch as I fought the urge to reach out and touch it. Not being a part of his orgasm felt like a loss, one that would help me remember my damn water in the future. "Yes, Sir. Can I have you before work tomorrow?"

"Yes. My good girl won't forget again, I know that." He picked me up, carrying me to the bedroom and laying me down on the edge of the bed and kissing all over my thighs to help me get in the mood. "Tell me two things you love about yourself. I won't be degrading you tonight, but the same concept applies. Even in punishment, I need you to be okay."

He lifted that shirt and forced my legs apart before I could answer, flicking his tongue almost angrily.

"I—" I struggled this time, not because I didn't want to give him what he desired, but because I was struggling to think about the things I loved about myself. "I love my … wit, and my ability to keep a poker face at work when I need to."

"Good girl." He backed off a little, sucking my clit just enough to make my stubborn body twitch, then slid two fingers inside of me. "Rock, beautiful."

I did as told, moaning and allowing myself to enjoy the pleasure I didn't deserve, even if Harrison would say otherwise. He was so fucking good with his tongue it didn't take long to get me where he wanted me, and when I came, I stilled my hips and gripped his hair.

He stayed there, peppering kisses between my thighs until I twitched and let him up, but he clicked his tongue to tell me not to move. "I want you, Briella. Having to touch myself when I have your mouth, your hands, your pussy and your ass right here and begging to be taken is fucking torture. I'm almost tempted not to waste the come if I can't breed you or fill up your throat, but what's done is done. Now sit up and watch."

As Harrison settled in the chair across from the bed and pulled himself out, I flinched with the need to go closer. *This will be the ultimate torture, is this how I made him feel back in that elevator? Before he caved and dropped down on his knees to taste me?* "So handsome, Sir. All of you."

That sinful tongue dragged slowly over his palm a moment before he began stroking himself, locking hooded, frustrated eyes with me. "Do you agree that you belong to me, Briella?"

"Yes, Sir. I'm yours." I pulled my knees to my chest and kept our gazes together. "All of me."

"Then you take care of what's mine," he muttered, pumping his hand faster and twisting until I could see his hips canting. "Do you understand?"

"Yes," I gasped, my hands tensing as I watched him get closer and closer to the edge. "I'll take care of what's yours, Sir. I'll be your good girl."

He tiptoed that line for what felt like hours — I could see the struggle, see how hard it was to tip himself over now when what he truly wanted was within his grasp, and I heard the frustrated grunt he let out when he finally came. He slumped, chest heaving and come ruining that open suit. "Then go get ready for bed. Our punishment is over."

Our.

With a nod, I went to do as told, and then that night I held him closer than ever. We were in this together, the good and the bad, and knowing me being forgetful also punished him was enough to have me setting a water reminder in my phone the next morning.

I woke him by kissing down his chest toward the cock I'd craved all night, and the moment he opened his eyes, he was shoving his cock down my throat. "Ten seconds, Briella. Then ride me."

I counted in my head and sucked him desperately until he was rock hard, then pulled off and straddled his lap, sinking down with a loud groan. "Thank you, Sir."

"Wait." He gripped my hip to stop me, then rolled slightly and stretched to grab my glasses and hand them to me. "Now."

He bucked up, making my hands drop down to his toned chest to hang on. I rode him slow and deep until his painful grip told me he couldn't take it anymore, and then I sped up rolling my hips in a way that drove him crazy. Within minutes he was dying, commanding me to come with a hand reaching to grip my throat. I thanked him with a raspy groan as I came all over his gorgeous dick and grinned when he instantly followed.

"My beautiful Briella," he purred, sliding his hand down over my stomach. "Think maybe it'll take this time?"

I couldn't stop the gasp that escaped, nor the life that flashed before my eyes, a life next to him. "I hope so, Sir."

"I still don't want you to tell me if you're on birth control or not," he admitted, tracing a circle over my belly button. "I'd rather be able to keep dreaming."

I smiled, leaning in to kiss along his jaw and burrow into his neck. "One day, baby. One day."

Vanilla

I could tell I'd been a good girl. Harrison has been spoiling me more than ever, and when he told me to come over to his house out of nowhere one Sunday afternoon, I knew I was in for a treat.

Nothing was out of the ordinary when I entered, there were no hints to what he had planned, and when I opened his bedroom door, I found no toys.

Just him, propped up on a couple of pillows with a book in his hand, a bare chest, and my favorite sweatpants. "No scenes today, Bri. I just want you." He set that book down and held out his arms, and I climbed into them without complaint.

I could have laid there with him forever. I felt safe, warm, wanted, all the things I'd craved for years, and Harrison was giving it to me. "You're comfy … and you smell good."

I moved my head into his armpit and inhaled, making him chuckle. "At least it's truer now than the last time you told me that," he commented. "I was starting to question your sense of smell."

"My sense of smell works just fine. I just like your scent … no matter what, apparently." I moved to see him better and smiled. "Did you miss me today?"

He nodded, leaning in to kiss my nose. "Yes. The Maduro trial starts tomorrow so I don't know how

much I'll see you for the next few
weeks, and I spent a little time earlier thinking back nostalgically about
how I used to dump all the work on
you."

I huffed, rolling my eyes at him
playfully. "You were a dick. You
don't do that anymore, but Grant
does now. I wouldn't mind helping
you more often instead of him."

"I'll kick his ass one day," he as-
sured me. "I nearly did last Thursday, I overheard him talking to Matt
about the dress you were wearing."

"Gross." But I smiled anyway, I
couldn't help it. "Made you want to
kick his ass, huh? Does it help that
he's never seen under my dress and
you have?"

"Entirely, yes. But I still wanted
to smash his face into the glass. It's
… hard for me not to retaliate,
though I respect your ability to fight

your own battles and defend your own honor. I'm being a good boy."

The thought of Harrison ever being a good boy had me biting back a laugh. "Is that so? Am I allowed to call you one?"

"If you value your life, I advise against it," he muttered. "Maybe that will be my punishment one day."

"Maybe." I leaned in for a kiss, lingering there for a long moment before breaking it. "I missed you too, by the way."

I watched his eyes close and his chest deflate as he relaxed, and I recognized the signs of trial nerves. Even the great Harrison Stag wasn't immune. "I'm glad you came," he whispered, sliding his hand up under my shirt to my skin. "Are you okay if we don't do a scene today?"

"Yes," I breathed, leaning in for another kiss as his touch lit my skin on fire. "You can still have me."

"Good." He flipped us both, taking his time undressing me and kissing all over my body. I could feel the affection with every press of those devilish lips, every swipe of his fingers over my skin, and when he finally got his fill of tasting me and slid inside me, he took his time there, too. "Mine," he whispered, voice void of its usual growl when he said things like that. "My beautiful Bri."

I wrapped my legs around him, not wanting his positioning to change. "Yours," I agreed. "All of me, every day if you wanted."

He drove himself deeper as he kissed over my neck, lazily rocking into me until I was digging my nails into his skin. "Every day, huh? Are you telling me you want to move in, Ms. Lewis?"

I couldn't lie to him, not while he was inside me and I was raw and open for him. "Yes, Sir."

"So do it. You already have a key, a drawer here, and I'm in possession of every sex toy you own. I would love to come home to you every day."

Those thrusts got sharper, but no faster, and knowing he would love it as much as I would had me feeling things I'd been trying not to think about. Falling for Harrison was scary. "I'd love that too. I love being here, I'd love being your live-in sex doll."

His teeth caught my lip. "No. Right now, you're not my sex doll. You're not my little slut, my whore, or anything else. You're Briella Lewis, a gorgeous woman I admire and respect, and you're not allowed to take that from me right now."

I gasped, body trembling with his words and the idea that he was falling just as hard as I was. I kissed him slowly, feeling the truth behind his words with each swipe of his tongue, and I was a goner.

Time blurred after that, as we rolled around and kissed more than actually moved. I'd never felt so much attention, so much affection, so much *intensity* from one man before — and I couldn't deny it anymore, I was in love with him. "Oh god, I'm gonna come. Harrison!"

I didn't hold back this time, I didn't wait for permission because that wasn't the type of sex we were having. We were making love, so I showed him exactly how good he made me feel when he showered me in all of him. I came with a gasp, clenching tightly around him, and he followed almost instantly like he'd been waiting for me.

"Bri," he whispered, burying it deeper and rolling his hips hard. "My Bri."

"Yours, only yours … I've been yours since that night in the elevator, Harrison. There's been no one else, I don't want anyone else. I just want you, all the time."

He slid out slowly and laid next to me, but his fingers instantly found my skin again. "I was serious, Briella. Move in. Don't get rid of your apartment yet, I don't want to leave you without options … but start staying here every day and we'll see how it goes. I might've been with other people, but I've been yours since the day you started at Brannigan Blake."

"Okay," I said with a smile. "I'll move in … does this mean we have to disclose our relationship to HR or something? I've never dated someone at work, let alone lived with one."

I'd never seen a smile appear and disappear so fast. "Probably. I know there are lines we'd have to tread, particularly if and when we work cases together. There are only two people in our HR department though, and I play poker every other Thursday with one of them. I'll see what I can find out before we make any decisions."

I nodded, desperately wanting that smile to return. "We don't have to tell anyone anything yet, okay? I kinda love having to sneak into your office sometimes."

"Good. Then we'll play that by ear," he agreed. "Go to your place after work tomorrow and pack what you need for the week, and then next weekend we'll get the rest."

"Already getting bossy again, aren't you?" I bit my lip and leaned in to bite his chin. "Will you kick me out if I move your shit around in the kitchen?" I bit him again, then gasped as he flipped and pinned my hands above my head.

"Unless you're going to start cooking for me every day, yes, I'm going to be cranky."

Him pinning my arms above my head was definitely in my list of top ten favorite things in the world. "But you're so sexy when you're cranky."

"Is that why you tested me for years?" he growled, biting the tip of my nose. "Bad girl."

I couldn't fight the guilty laugh that escaped. "It was for my spank bank … now I get the real deal."

"Mhm. Only you."

Somehow, I knew this moment would live in my head forever. The thought of being able to wake up to him every morning had a permanent smile on my face, and knowing he was all mine had me happier than ever. I loved this soft side of Harrison, a side I knew hardly anyone in the world got to see. I also knew *I* wouldn't see this side often, but that was what made it so damn special.

He'd be back to spanking me again in no time.

Cockwarming

My first official day of living with Harrison, he woke me up with kisses all over my face and neck, and when my eyes focused on his face, I instantly knew he wanted to play. "Morning, Sir."

"Good morning, beautiful. How'd you sleep?" Those kisses continued, making words difficult as I bared my neck.

"Slept perfect. You?" I asked, running my fingernails down his back softly.

"Fantastic. And now I want to eat breakfast with my cock buried in your throat." He bit me there, then pulled back with a devilish smile. "How long do you think you could cockwarm for me if I was praising you?"

"Until the end of time," I said without a trace of doubt. "Can I keep you warm all day, Sir? Breakfast, watching TV, working in your office. Let me show you how much I mean it."

His lips danced over my jaw as he thought about that, then nodded. "Not until the end of time, but yes. We'll see how long you can last. You've got a half hour to do whatever you need to do, and when you're done, come meet me downstairs. Deal?"

"Deal." I kissed his cheek and went to brush my teeth and tie up my hair. I went with no clothes and glasses and scarfed down some breakfast before I turned to face him. "I'm ready, Sir."

He already had his breakfast laid out as he slid back his chair and sat down, patting his thigh. "Good girl. You look stunning like this ... now get on your knees."

I dropped down like the good little slut I was and awaited further directions. I loved this, loved the thrill of him putting me on my knees like I wasn't the strong, independent woman that I was, because with him ... I didn't have to be.

"That's my girl," he crooned. "Get me hard first while you tell me one thing you love about being a sub."

I reached up to stroke him with our eyes locked. "I was just thinking about that, Sir. I love how light it makes me feel, like I don't have to be Briella Lewis, paralegal who fought tooth and nail for everything in her life. I can just breathe. You take all the weight off my shoulders, and you call me a good girl for it. I love everything about being a sub. Everything about being yours to break and make new, because every time you put me back together, I feel stronger than before."

"Good. Then let me break you, kitten. Open wide."

His thumb hooked the base of his length and he pushed forward, grazing my lips until I opened for him fully and let him in. The hiss, the clenching thighs, the grip he had on my hair were all worth the immediate stretch to my jaw, but nothing felt quite as good as the praise he let freely drip from his lips.

"Mouth feels like heaven, Briella. You look so good down there on your knees for me. Suck just a little and then stay still," he commanded. "Be my good girl."

11 SCENES

I wanted to be his good girl, needed it like I needed air, so I suckled just enough to make him twitch and then relaxed my muscles, eyes flickering closed as I sat there at his mercy.

His fork clanked against his plate as he started to eat and whisper praises between bites. I knew he couldn't see me from my spot underneath that table, but his fingers threaded mindlessly through my hair as he sat hot and heavy in my mouth, and I drifted further into that comfortable, weightless headspace I craved so much.

"Good girl," he whispered. "My perfect, beautiful Briella. Does your jaw hurt yet?"

I gently shook my head no, suckling once just to show him I was okay and then let myself slip right back into subspace. Time moved slower there, like it was just Harrison and I in the world and nothing bad would ever happen to either of us.

Until his phone rang, anyway.

"Ethan," Harrison said, all husky and inconvenienced. "This isn't really a good time."

His brother. Oh, hell.

I couldn't hear the voice on the other end, but whatever he said made Harrison huff, and something told me he guessed exactly what was happening. I stayed put like the good little slut I was and focused back on the husband-dick inside my throat.

"So tell one of the twins. I'm not the only brother you have, and it's about time one of them volunteers as tribute. I'm in the middle of a trial anyway, I can't." His free hand tightened in my hair and started moving my head, just slowly at first. "Great. Go do your mind tricks on someone else, my head is otherwise occupied."

I heard his phone clatter back to the table as he let out a breath and started fucking my face. I kept my throat relaxed as he took what he needed from me, hoping that if he came he'd still make me stay right here attached to him when he was done, and I wasn't disappointed — he barely let me off him for the time it took him to come all over my cheeks, and I was right back where I started.

The rest of the day went more or less the same, with short little breaks for me to use the restroom, eat and drink. Other than that, I had Harrison Stag's cock in my mouth whether he was even hard or not, and by his third orgasm, I was sore as hell and struggling to keep my eyes open, even with how wet I was between my legs. I managed to get my eyes open to meet his, hoping he'd see how gone I was without me having to tap out, and he did.

"Up, beautiful." He helped me climb into his lap and held me, kissing lightly all over my cheek. "You were incredible. Always so good for me, Briella. My good little slut takes my cock so well in all her holes."

I melted into him, soaking up all his praise and attention. "I'm yours, Sir. I was made for you." My jaw ached, knees were screaming, but everything else about me was perfectly content to be his little slut forever.

"Then tell me how you want to come, beautiful. It's your choice, you've earned that."

I shifted my weight just slightly so I was straddling his thigh and then rolled my hips. "Like this, Sir. Please keep kissing my face and neck, it feels so good."

"You got it, kitten. Come when you're ready." Those strong arms held me up and helped me move as his lips and tongue explored my skin, and knowing I had all of his attention had my head falling back with a gasp as we found a rhythm. My clit was throbbing in minutes, his sweats soaked where I was grinding down hard, and when I came I let his name fall from my lips seconds before I caught him in a deep kiss.

He had me lifted up and in the shower upstairs like it was nothing, and the constant stream of kisses and validations had me weak. By the time we were wrapped up in our bed again with his leg looped over mine to pin me there, I was spent — but he wasn't quite done with me yet.

"Tell me one toy you've always been curious about but never got to try," he whispered, peppering kisses over my face again. "Anything at all. I want to … watch this weekend."

"Um …" I took my time to consider his question, not wanting to rush and blurt out something I'd want to take back after, and when I thought about the porn I enjoyed, I actually blushed. "Well, I've always wanted to try a sex machine, but that was before you. I know no machine could fuck me as good as you do."

"No machine will ever fuck you as well as a human will, but I admire your choice. Sleep now, beautiful. We'll talk about it more tomorrow and discuss how it will go."

"Thank you, Sir. Goodnight." I'd had some pretty lame lays when I was younger, but I wasn't in a position to argue with him.

We'd find out that weekend, anyway.

The Machine

Harrison

Saturday afternoon, I spoiled her. I wasn't sure if that word really meant anything anymore since I did my best to treat her like a queen on a daily basis – but better than, since I never punished her for having a mind of her own. This scene was different though and required a little more finesse to pull it off, so I doted.

Breakfast in bed, an early-morning bubble bath, a full body massage as she dried off on a giant, fluffy towel. Touching her was a gift I was taking seriously, especially when I considered the scene we had planned.

I wouldn't be able to touch her at all until she asked for me.

What fucking torture.

In the hours leading up to our scene, I kept her within reach. Always close enough to touch, to smell, always in sight. It still felt surreal having her here at all, and though I wasn't handling our transition at work as well as I could've been, I was damned grateful to finally have her. I'd do anything to keep her.

Anything.

"Are you ready?" I asked, kissing her nose and leading her downstairs when it was finally time. "You'll still use 'Blizzard' as your safeword, but remember you chose 'Colder' as your codeword when you're done

143

with that machine and ready for me. I'll be able to hear you from the other room, and the camera is facing directly at the bed. I'll see you, too. You'll never be in danger, Briella. All you'll need to do is say the word and I'll be in here."

"I trust you, Sir."

"Good girl. Then let's begin."

I carried her to the foot of the bed and laid her down, then stole a few more kisses from her as I positioned her legs in the stirrups and secured her arms above her head. Already, she looked so sinfully hot that I almost called off the whole thing to take her just like that — spread open for me and completely unable to stop me from claiming her, all of her, until I'd finally had my fill.

Instead, I reminded myself that I'd have her before the night was through and doublechecked that she was comfortable. My vision was fucking blurry from how turned on I was as I started that machine just to watch her twitch at the sound, and I played with the buttons on the remote for it to test the speeds and how far it thrust. The last thing I ever wanted to do was hurt her, so I made sure I positioned it far enough away that it wouldn't ruin her.

Not completely, anyway.

I lubed that silicone cock that I was trying not to be jealous of and let her listen to me stroke it for a minute just to get her in the mood. "Hear this, kitten? That'll be me soon enough, watching you on a camera as this thing takes you apart. Do you want this inside of you now? Tell me. I need to hear my good little whore say she wants to have her pussy wrecked by a machine."

"I want it, Sir. I want that fake cock to tear me apart and drive you crazy."

"Good girl. Blizzard and Colder. Remember those, and I'll see you soon. I'll be edging for you, but you have my full permission to come as many times as you need to. Just call me when you're ready." I kissed her again, then nudged that dick inside her with the machine off. There wouldn't be a chance in Hell that I could stay away if we started now, so I ducked quickly out of the room with the remote in my hand and settled in front of the small monitor I'd set up for this.

Once I tested the two-way audio to make sure we wouldn't have a problem hearing each other, I took a deep breath and started the machine.

"Oh, fuck," she breathed, rolling her hips a little as she got used to the movement. "That's ... that's not bad. Definitely not you."

"Of course it's not. But don't let that stop you, kitten. My good little slut doesn't care what's stuffing her full, does she? She just loves to be filled."

"Fuck yes!"

I watched her for what felt like an hour, just taking that thing and tugging at the ropes tying her wrists to the headboard. I couldn't handle how gorgeous she was, how eagerly she was taking that long, thick cock that was easily twice my size. I played with the speed and intensity until she was gasping, twitching in those stirrups and squirming on the bed, and it just about killed me.

I grunted, pulling my aching, straining cock out of my sweats and fumbling with the lube. Seeing her like this, spread out and taking that thing ... it was better than any porno I'd ever seen, better than any show at any club I'd ever been to. "Fucking hell, Briella. You're such a good girl, such a good *fucking* girl … ride it. Ride it like you'd ride me," I rushed out, knowing that wouldn't really be possible thanks to her position — but she surprised me like always. She used the leverage the stirrups provided and rolled her gorgeous hips, so I slowed the speed to help her out and gripped the base of my own cock so I wouldn't hit the edge too fast.

She gasped. "Holy shit, I … I think I'm gonna come."

So much for that.

"Do it, kitten. Come. Over and over again until your legs don't want to work anymore and you can't fucking see straight. Show me how much you love being used by a fucking *machine.*"

"Fuck me running, that feels so fucking good, fas—harder, please! Sir!"

I turned the speed up and watched it fuck her through that first orgasm, then the second one, too. My breaths were coming in ragged, desperate, ridiculous bursts as I stood, practically pressing my nose to that monitor and only touching myself enough to keep me walking that line between pleasure and torture.

"Oh god, I c— Harrison!"

"So good, Briella, my beautiful girl. Do you have any fucking idea what you're doing to me right now? How hard I am for you, how badly I want to come in there and fuck you until you bleed?"

Her gorgeous body bowed with those words as she moaned loudly, coming a third time on that silicone cock, and she was so fucking wet that it slipped right out of her and was rubbing her clit now instead of fucking her soaked pussy. "Harrison!"

"Damnit," I hissed, grabbing the remote again and squeezing the hell out of my cock as I kicked my sweats the rest of the way off and ran back in there. As much as I wanted her then, she still hadn't said the word, so I dropped the remote next to her ass and guided the dildo back inside of her. "Keep taking it, kitten. Seeing it in person is so much fucking better than on a screen … and now I can touch you."

I slapped her clit and the inside of her thighs, over and over, harder and harder until she was screaming and squirting and forcing the dildo out of her again. It was by far the hottest thing I'd ever seen in my life, and I struggled to remain upright as she finally said it.

"Har— Sir ... Colder."

My foot connected to the stand that machine was on before I could think twice about it and kicked it out of the way, making room for me to slide fully between her parted legs. "One thing you love about yourself, Briella. Now."

I feverishly kissed the spots I'd slapped as she rattled off *three* things for me, and only then did I allow myself to push inside her. "God, Briella. I've never been inside such a hot, wet fucking slut before. Gonna breed your wrecked little cunt ... tell me you want it, tell me you need to feel me fill up your s— fu—"

It hit me harder than I expected. I gripped her hips hard, lifting her ass off the bed to angle as deep as I could, to make her take every fucking inch of my throbbing, pulsing cock as I came inside her, and the sound and heat and tight squeeze of her orgasm had me fucking that come deeper and growling as I willed it to finally take, birth control be damned.

One fucking day … I *would* see her carrying my child.

"Sir …"

The sound of her voice all weak like that had me pulling out instantly and unbinding her, and if I thought what I'd done for her that morning was spoiling, it was nothing compared to the way I treated her after.

She wasn't just a queen, she was a goddess, my own personal gift from whatever Heaven favored bastards like me … and if it was within my power at all, I'd never let her forget that.

Not ever.

The Aftercare

I let my head fall back against his shoulder with a sigh. I was done, so done, and he was the only thing keeping me tethered to Earth. I needed to feel as much of him as I could to stay awake. Harrison rarely ever got inside the bath with me, but after that last play session it was as if he knew I needed those touches. "Thank you," I whispered, hoping that he knew I meant for everything.

"I should be the one thanking you, Briella. Don't ever think that I don't understand what a gift you are." He trailed a palm full of water and bubbles up my skin, then tilted my face toward his to kiss him. "Because I do."

I smiled before our lips met, then stared into his gorgeous blue eyes. "A gift meant only for you. Just like you were for me."

"I need you to tell me five things you love about yourself. I know you told me one during the scene, but I know how intense that was. Please humor me."

"You're killing me with those," I said with a soft smile, because I really did love how much he cared. "My toes are pretty cute, cheekbones are nice, my handwriting, my inability to let go of the things I want, my love for you."

It was the closest I'd ever gotten to saying the words, and the way his hand stilled and his breathing hitched told me he understood.

JENSEN

"Say it, Briella."

Those three little words spilled out of me like they belonged to him and not me. "I love you. I love you, Harrison, and you don't have to say it back yet because I know in the scheme of things we haven't been together that long and have hardly been on dates like other couples. But I know what I feel, and because of what we share, I know it's real and raw and everything I should be scared to feel, but I do. I love you."

"Fuck that. I love you too. It's been months, Bri. It's not too soon, and 'too soon' doesn't exist, anyway," he whispered. "This is real."

I spun around to straddle his waist and kiss him, bubble-covered fingers running through his hair. It was real, everything with him was real, and I felt the truth of his words over every inch of my body.

155

He kissed me until I was light-headed and almost giddy, then broke it just long enough to spin me around again and actually clean me. Every touch, every ghost of his lips, every gentle, tender graze of his fingertips had me falling deeper, and I found myself grateful that I lived with him now. I'd never have to go to sleep without him.

"Are you hungry? You need water, at least, but probably food too."

"Yes, but I want a giant cinnamon roll with extra glaze." I peeked back to smile at him. "Can we order in and just cuddle?"

"Absolutely, and I'll even try really hard not to point out that right now, you're the cinnamon roll with extra glaze. And I'm not sorry." He chuckled, helping me out of the tub and wrapping a towel around me. "Tonight and tomorrow, though, you can have whatever you want. You've earned it."

"Whatever I want, huh?" I went on my toes to kiss his scruffy jaw. "And if I just want you and junk food, that's okay?"

He nodded as he helped me dry off. "Encouraged, actually. Surprisingly, I find it attractive when you devour an entire package of Oreos in one sitting. Just keep those glasses on and you could get away with murder for the next twenty-four hours."

"Noted, Mr. Stag. All I need is my glasses." My kisses changed to one quick bite and then I spun around to comb out my hair. "You spoil me, baby."

"It's funny that you use that word. I thought so too, but I realized that was disingenuous of me. I really don't spoil you. I treat you exactly the same way that every man should treat their partner, especially when their partner is such a good girl."

Not even the teasing tone he adopted at the end could dull the words, and I let my eyes close and allowed my body to feel them. "Thank you, Sir. Extra frosting so I can lick some of it off your cock later."

He twitched, hard. "A very, *very* good girl."

He stuck to his word. Harrison ensured I ate a good meal, drank a fuckton of water, and then put about ten pillows around us when we finally settled down on our couch. He nuzzled me in with the biggest cinnamon roll I'd ever seen, and although he said he wasn't … I was definitely feeling very spoiled. And I loved it. "I'm glad you like me just as much when I'm not in makeup and heels."

"I happen to like you in all your forms, and to be honest, I'm a little relieved when you take your makeup off and won't get foundation all over my shirts when you try to smell my armpits out of nowhere," he teased. "I wish I'd have known three years ago that you were into that sort of thing. Would've made torturing you easier."

"That's a secret, you signed a contract not to disclose that information to anyone the moment you bred me. Them's the rules." I blushed anyway, feeling caught and called out but not judged in the slightest.

"Your secrets are all safe with me, kitten. For the record, I think you're gorgeous with or without makeup. The effort you put in isn't lost on me."

I held out a bite for him and then took one for myself, getting frosting on my chin in the process. I couldn't help but laugh at the fact that this handsome, powerful man was calling me gorgeous while I sat in front of him with messy hair and frosting on my chin, but I believed him with all of me. "So when we started, you said something about a trial run … are we past that now? Do you believe we are compatible?"

"Yes, I do," he admitted. "I've never been with someone I'm more compatible with. Sure, we still have our differences, but I think that makes it even better. I will say though, that it's important to me to have days where we break from our typical dynamic. I don't mean switching, I mean days when we simply don't fall into that power dynamic. I still need you to be the feisty, fiery woman who drove me insane for a decade. I want days where I can be soft with you and let you be a brat without feeling the need to punish you. And sometimes, I just want to have regular, boring old sex with you because I can't keep my damn hands off of you. And I've also realized that I'm not okay with degrading you outside of the bedroom, which you mentioned being interested in at some point."

"No, I don't think I'm interested in that anymore. Now that I know how good it feels in a closed setting, I don't think I would handle it as well outside. I think we're more on the same page than we ever thought we would be. I loved vanilla sex with you, Harrison."

"Then yes. I think we're perfectly compatible. I suppose it's a good thing I've already given you a key." He kissed my nose and held me closer. "Mine, Briella. My beautiful Bri."

"All yours, all of me." When our lips met I felt all the promise in the world behind it, and I couldn't wait to see what the future held for us.

Harrison Fucking Stag was mine.

Also By
Octavia Jensen

BOYS OF BRISLEY:
King Hunt
Exposed King

ELEVEN:
11 Hours
11 Scenes
11 Dates
Sin Sessions

WHITECREST:
Business & Pleasure
Eyes On Me
Can't You See
Over A Cliff
Motocross My Heart
Rose-Colored Boy

BURNING RIVER:
Santa's Lay
All Over You
Heels Over Head
Just Like This

STANDALONES:
Don't Go
Take Me Twice

VISIT OCTAVIA JENSEN AT

www.celiketchpublishing.com/
octaviajensen
Or check her out on social media!

Facebook: Author Octavia Jensen
Instagram: @authoroctaviajensen
TikTok: @authoroctaviajensen

Printed in Great Britain
by Amazon